Steven Spielberg Presents

An American Tail: Fievel Goes West ™

The Novelization

**Adapted by Cathy East Dubowski
From a screenplay by Flint Dille
Story by Charles Swenson
Based upon characters created by
David Kirschner**

Grosset & Dunlap · New York

1

Another Night with No Cheese

Daylight was fading on Hester Street. In a tiny dark apartment, Mama Mousekewitz gently laid her baby Yasha in a homemade cradle and began to make dinner.

"Another night with no cheese," Mama said sadly as she set the table.

Just then Papa came in the door. Mama looked up hopefully. Papa just shook his head.

Papa Mousekewitz was a violin maker. All day long he had tried to sell his precious violins so he could buy food for his family. But no one had any money.

America. New York City. 1884. It was not at all like they had dreamed it would be.

Once the Mousekewitz family had lived in a tiny village in Russia. There was Papa, Mama, Tanya, Fievel, and baby Yasha. They had been poor. And always, always there were the cats to fear.

But Papa had heard tales of America. A mouse hole in every wall! Bread crumbs on every floor!

And best of all, said Papa, in America there were *no cats!*

Papa wanted a better life for his family. He decided it was time to leave.

And so the Mousekewitz family began the long hard journey to America.

But thousands of other mice left their homelands, too. Hundreds and hundreds of mice poured into New York City, hoping to find that better life.

The mice came with few belongings. Most could barely speak English. It was hard to find work. It was hard to find a place to live. And now most of them—just like the Mousekewitz family—were poorer than before. And worst of all . . .

America was *full* of cats!

But neither cats nor poverty could stop the music that filled eight-year-old Tanya's heart. Tonight she sat on the windowsill of the Mousekewitzes' tiny apartment singing a beautiful song—a song that made all their problems seem to disappear. Mama and Papa smiled proudly at their daughter. But not everyone liked Tanya's singing.

"Hey! How about a little peace and quiet!" shouted a mouse in the next apartment building.

Tanya had just come to her favorite part, so she kept singing. Her voice soared like a bird above the dirty crowded streets. She hit a very high note—

Crash! Tanya covered her ears at the sound of breaking glass.

"Hey!" growled the man in the next building. "Your singing broke my mirror!" Tanya ducked as the man threw a tomato at her. It splattered the windowsill like ketchup.

A lady next to him threw an overripe peach. SPLAT!

"Papa!" cried Tanya. "They're throwing fruit and vegetables at me!"

"Keep singing!" said Papa as he caught the fruit. "Maybe we'll have enough for dessert!"

Mama went to the window and stuck her head out over the street. "Fievel! Fievel Mousekewitz!" she called. "Your supper's ready. Fievel . . ."

Seven-year-old Fievel Mousekewitz was on a rooftop, just a few blocks down the street. But he might as well have been a hundred miles away. Fievel didn't hear his mother calling or his sister singing. He didn't see the people bartering noisily with the vendors on the street below. He was busy reading an old paperback book, a human-sized novel he had found in the trash. It was a tale of Sheriff Wylie Burp and the American West: Cowboys! Outlaws! Showdowns at sunset!

But Fievel wasn't just reading. He was dreaming he was really out West. He was pretending to be a famous gunslinger. And only Fievel Mousekewitz could save Sheriff Burp!

"Wylie Burp looked across the dusty street," Fievel read from the book. "The Cactus Cat Gang had him surrounded. But the sheriff would never back down . . ."

Fievel jumped from a stack of old crates. "Have no fear!" he cried. "Fievel the Kid is here!"

"It's too tough, Kid," said Sheriff Burp. "Get out while you can!"

"No way," said Fievel. "If you're biting the dust, I'm going down with you."

Fievel joined the fight. Minutes later, the Cactus Cat Gang was running for the desert.

"You saved my life, Kid," said the sheriff. "I'll never forget it." Then he pinned a shiny tin star on Fievel's shirt.

Suddenly Sheriff Burp gaped at something beyond Fievel's shoulder. "Look out behind you, Kid!"

Fievel spun around, guns in the air.

"Fievel! Your supper's ready!"

The voice of Fievel's mother broke the spell. His daydream faded. The Western town became Hester Street again. Wylie Burp disappeared.

But a real cat was charging straight for him!

4

2
Cat Attack

Fievel didn't run. He stood his ground as the cat screeched to a stop right in front of him.

Then Fievel smiled. "Hi, Tiger!" he said.

Tiger was a sweet, soft-hearted cat. He actually liked mice—but not to eat. Tiger was a vegetarian, and he and Fievel had become the best of friends.

Today Tiger looked upset. "Fievel!" he cried. "Have you seen her?"

"Seen who, Tiger?"

"Miss Kitty, who else?"

Fievel looked across the street to a red-brick building. A beautiful well-dressed cat was coming down the fire escape. She had a suitcase in her paw.

"There she is," said Fievel. "But you'd better hurry. It looks as if she's going somewhere."

Then Fievel heard his mother calling him again.

"See you later, Tiger," Fievel said and he headed for home, smiling as he watched Tiger run toward the kitty he loved.

"Miss Kitty, wait!" cried Tiger. "Where are you going?"

Miss Kitty smiled kindly at Tiger. "I've got a ticket out West," she said. "A ticket to the land of sunshine. I heard there's a town out there that promises a new way of life. And a brand-new breed of cat."

"What's wrong with my breed?" asked Tiger.

Miss Kitty sighed. "Look, Tiger. I don't mean to be mean. You're a wonderful cat. But you're a bit of a fraidy-cat. City cats just don't have enough growl in their howl for me. I want . . . How shall I put it? I want a cat who's more like a dog."

"But Miss Kitty—"

The sound of wagon wheels and horses' hooves clattered down the street.

"That's my ride out West," said Miss Kitty. "Good-bye, Tiger." She picked up her suitcase. And with a swirl of skirts, she jumped into the wagon below.

Miss Kitty blew Tiger one last kiss as the wagon carried her down the crowded street. The heart-broken cat tried to be brave. He waved until he could no longer see her.

Then Tiger broke down and cried.

At the Mousekewitz home, dinner was on the table. Mama was just about to call Fievel again.

Suddenly the door slammed open. Fievel swaggered in like a cowboy rolling into a saloon.

"Howdy Ma! Where's the grub?"

"Fievel!" Mama cried. "Where have you been? You're late for supper."

"I had to save Sheriff Wylie Burp!" he said. "The Cactus Cat Gang was after him and—"

Mama grabbed Fievel by his tail. "Such a tall tale, Fievel. And dirty hands, too? Go wash."

"Oh, Mama! I just washed," Fievel said. "Last week!" Mama gave him a warning look, and he hurried to wash his hands. Then he joined his family at the table.

But Fievel saw that Papa was not eating. He was staring at the violins that covered the wall.

"In Russia my violins were famous," Papa said sadly. "We were poor, but we never went hungry." He looked at the simple supper on his family's table. "Now we don't even have enough food . . ."

Fievel gave his sister a playful push. "Maybe Tanya should sing some more."

"Very funny!" said Tanya. She made a face. "You'll see. One day I'll be a big singing star. People will come from miles around—"

"Yeah," said Fievel, giggling. "To eat!"

But even the children's teasing chatter could not cheer Papa tonight.

"Fievel's birthday will be soon." Papa choked back tears. "I don't even have money for presents."

"Oh, Papa!" cried Fievel. "I don't care."

"I could always sing in front of the gift shop," said Tanya. "Maybe they'd throw presents!"

7

This time everyone laughed—even Papa. "How lucky I am to have such fine children!" he said.

Suddenly an alarm sounded! Fievel and Tanya covered their ears. Baby Yasha began to cry. Papa ran to the window to see what was wrong.

"Cat attack! Cat attack!" a mouse shouted from the street.

3

A Narrow Escape

Hester Street was filled with cats! They pounced on crates and boxes. They pawed at tiny mouse windows. The frightened mice fled from their homes, down into the sewer. They were searching for someplace to hide.

Down the street Tiger stopped in his tracks. He heard howls and meows and squeaks. "The mice!" he cried. "I've got to help them!"

Jumping from rooftop to rooftop, Tiger ran toward the noise. Then he saw an elegant cat named Cat R. Waul smiling wickedly as he gave out orders to attack. Beside him sat an inky black spider with glowing red eyes.

"A sp-sp-sp a tarantula!" cried Tiger. He fainted dead away in a swirl of stars and fell from the fire escape. Crash! Tiger landed in a trash can. The lid spun in the air then fell back in place, trapping Tiger inside.

At the Mousekewitz home, Mama snatched Yasha from her cradle and held her close. "We've got to hide!" she cried. Then they heard loud shouts from the street. Fievel ran to the window and looked outside. Hester Street was in shambles. And all because of the cats.

"Why, those no-good varmints!" he shouted. And he disappeared out the window.

"Fievel!" shouted Papa. "Come back!"

Fievel stuck his head back inside.

"Thank heavens!" said Papa.

Fievel grinned. "Forgot my hat!" he said, reaching through the window. He folded it into the shape of a cowboy hat. Then he charged down the fire escape into the streets. "Never fear! Fievel the Kid is here!"

A moment later another face appeared at the window. A huge furry face. This time it wasn't Fievel. It was a cat!

Hissing, the cat swatted at the mice through the tiny window. But he couldn't reach them. Snarling, he ripped the window right out of the wall.

"Come on!" said Papa. "Let's get out of here!" Hoping to find a safe place, the Mousekewitzes fled to the roof. But a snarling one-eyed cat was right behind them. He smacked his lips as he crept up on Mama and Tanya.

Suddenly a voice stopped the cat cold.

"Looks like you're missin' an eye, cat." Fievel stood on the edge of the roof like a hero in a Western novel. He pulled his hat down over one eye. "Now—this makes it a fair fight."

One-Eye didn't make a move. He just stared at Fievel. He had never been insulted by a mouse before.

"That's right, big guy," said Fievel. "I'm talkin' to you." He took a step toward the cat.

"Fievel!" screamed Mama. "Run for your life!"

Fievel looked up into the cat's one evil eye. He gulped as he stared at the cat's sharp glistening teeth. Fievel the cowboy hero turned back into Fievel the tiny mouse. "Eek!"

The cat stalked him into a corner. Fievel shook as the cat's paw swooped down on him.

SCREECH! The cat shut his eyes and covered his ears with his paws. He turned around. Where was that awful sound coming from?

It was Papa. He was playing high piercing notes on his violin. "Run, Fievel!" he cried.

Fievel dashed through the cat's legs. He jumped into an old tuna can that was lying on its side. One-Eye swatted the can and it started to roll.

"Everybody! Get in!" Fievel shouted. Papa, Tanya, and Mama—still holding baby Yasha—all jumped in as the can rolled past. The tin rolled away from the cat . . .

And off the edge of the roof! It bounced from the fire escape to a stack of boxes to the street. Then it began to roll down the center of Hester Street, with One-Eye right behind it.

But the can was losing speed. Slowly it rolled up

to a sewer grating and teetered on the edge. Papa peeked outside. One-Eye was closing in!

"Run!" shouted Papa.

But the Mousekewitzes didn't run *out* of the can. They ran inside. The can began to spin like a treadmill in a hamster's cage. At last it slipped through the grates, leaving One-Eye swiping at thin air.

"Jolly good," said the elegant Cat R. Waul, coming up behind him.

The mice had rolled right into his trap!

4

The Stranger

Far below Hester Street the Mousekewitz family tumbled into the dark waters of the sewer. At first the mice cheered their good luck—they had escaped from the cats!

But soon their tiny tin boat began to pitch and turn. The waters swelled into a raging river.

Suddenly Tanya screamed. They were heading straight toward a waterfall! The Mousekewitzes held each other tight as the boat swirled through the churning waves and crashed over the edge. "Yippee!" squealed Fievel as the boat plunged deep into the water and turned over.

The mice got a good dunking. But finally the boat righted itself. Mama, Papa, and Tanya sighed with relief.

Fievel's eyes, though, were shining. "What a ride!" he cried. "Let's go again!" Mama and Papa just shook their heads as the boat floated on into the darkness.

At last candlelight flickered up ahead. Eerie shadows danced upon the ceiling as the tin boat drifted toward a landing. A row of cardboard shacks leaned sadly against one wall.

In front of the houses a crowd of mice had gathered. They were listening breathlessly to a strange mouse dressed in a cowboy suit. He held one stiff arm above his head and waved a fistful of tickets.

"Pardon me, my fine mice friends," said the stranger. "But I am in need of help." The ragged city mice looked at one another in surprise. How could they help this cowboy mouse?

"It seems I have some train tickets out West. Tickets to the land of sunshine—which I will be unable to use. Surely some of you are looking for a little more room?"

No one said a word.

"Ah. I was afraid of that," said the stranger. "The mice here in New York have everything they need. Lots of space," he glanced at the shacks crowded together, "and lots of cheese. None of you would be interested in a place where cheese grows on trees."

"Cheese trees! I'm interested!" shouted one mouse as he pushed his way to the front of the crowd. "I'll take one of them tickets!"

"I'll take them all!" a mouse behind him cried.

The crowd pressed forward. Everyone held out money for tickets.

"No need to push," the stranger said. He pulled out a long roll of tickets. "There's plenty for everybody." The mice were too excited to wonder why he had so many tickets.

But one woman did have a question. She trembled as she asked, "Hey, mister—are there any cats out West?"

The sewer fell silent as each mouse strained to hear.

"There are cats, all right," he said. "But out West the cats and mice are friends."

The mice stared in amazement.

"That's right," said the stranger. "In fact, cats even get along with dogs out there. Why, Sheriff Burp is the best-known law dog in the West!"

Fievel's eyes lit up. "Wylie Burp! Papa, let's go."

"No more nights without cheese," said Mama.

"Maybe they like singers out there!" said Tanya.

Papa looked at his family. Once again their eyes were full of hope. How could he say no?

Papa pulled a small bag from his pocket. It held all the money the Mousekewitzes had. But he gave it eagerly to the stranger. And the stranger handed him five very special tickets.

Tickets to a brand-new life!

The Mousekewitz family joined in as the crowd of mice laughed and talked of their future out West. No one looked very closely at the stranger. They didn't see the strings tied to his arms and legs— strings that led up through the sewer grate to the street above.

No one guessed that the strange mouse was, in fact, a wooden puppet.

And no one saw who was pulling the puppet's strings: the grinning Cat R. Waul, with Chula the spider by his side.

5

Train to Green River

The next day Tiger the cat walked along Hester Street. He couldn't believe all the destruction. Well, he thought sadly, spend one night in a garbage can and look what happens. Little mouse houses lay torn apart. Shops stood open, their goods scattered onto the sidewalk. Where were the mice?

Tiger ran to the building where Fievel lived. Frightened, he looked in the window. The apartment was dark and empty. Bits of broken violin littered the floor.

"Oh, no!" moaned Tiger. He poked his head inside for a better view—and his head got stuck! Before Tiger could wiggle it loose, he saw a note lying on the table in the middle of the room.

Dear Tiger,
    We have left New York. We are taking the train to a town out West called Green River. I tried to find you to tell you. But I guess you were off somewhere with Miss Kitty. I

miss you, Tiger. I hope I see you again sometime.

Your best friend,
Fievel

Tiger pulled his head loose from the window. Then he sat down on the curb and sighed. New York City was his home. He'd never even been anywhere else. But now Fievel and Miss Kitty were gone. Suddenly New York City was a very lonely place.

There was only one thing to do. Tiger ran toward the train station. He was going to follow his friends out West.

A huge black train sat on the tracks huffing steam. People and mice poured from the station to get on board.

"I'm sure we forgot something," Mama said, looking through their things. "Let's see, violins, pots and pans, the tail curler, the cheese board and knife . . ."

"Don't worry," said Papa. "It's going to be wonderful."

The human conductor pulled out his pocket watch. The mouse conductor climbed down the chain to check the time. "Last call! All passengers bound for Altoona, Akron, Oskaloosa, and . . . Greeeen River!"

Fievel stood at the edge of the platform and gave New York one long last look. "Bye, Tiger, wherever you are," he said sadly. "You were the best cat I ever met."

The train whistle blew and Papa pulled Fievel onto the train.

"All aboard!" shouted the human conductor.

"All aboard!" shouted the mouse conductor.

The train to Green River began to rumble out of the station. The Mousekewitz family was on its way out West!

But where was Tiger? The train was almost gone when Tiger shoved his way through the crowd. A pack of growling dogs had been chasing him all through the city. So he had two reasons for wanting to catch the train.

Now Tiger raced along the tracks with the dogs nipping at his heels. He leapt onto the back rail of the caboose just as one dog snapped at his backside.

Tiger stood at the railing gasping for breath. He was on the train! Sure, he had left some fur behind. But he had made it! "Stupid dog!" he shouted as the train pulled away. "Your mother was never housebroken!"

Then he turned to go inside—and came face to face with the snarling jaws of the train's fire dog.

"Yikes," Tiger mumbled. The dog had heard everything he said! Without another thought, Tiger leapt off the train just as it crossed over a bridge.

With a splash, he landed in the river below. Fievel and the train sped out West. And Tiger began to swim.

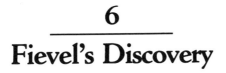

6

Fievel's Discovery

"Are we out West yet?"

Fievel asked his mama that question about once an hour as the train to Green River rumbled steadily along the tracks.

Mama smiled and shook her head. "It will take days and days to get there," she told him.

The mice passed the time singing songs about their new life as Fievel pressed his nose to the window and watched the whole country rush by. To him, America was the busy crowded neighborhoods of New York City.

But now Fievel saw acres of farmland dotted with herds of black and white dairy cows. He saw miles and miles of uncut forest without a building in sight. Magnificent mountains rose up against the colors of the setting sun.

The train chugged on as darkness fell. Never in New York had the moon seemed so huge, never had the stars seemed so bright. Wishes made on these glittering stars, thought Fievel, were bound to come true.

One by one the mice families said good night. Soon the steady rocking of the train lulled them to sleep.

But Fievel was wide awake. He was too excited to sleep. And he had a whole train to explore!

Quietly he slipped from his bed. He wandered from one train car to the next, poking into corners, peeking through cracks. One car was filled with dozing cattle. So Fievel scurried along a ceiling beam to get to the next car.

Then, up ahead, Fievel saw a faint light. He hurried along the beam. What was going on? Suddenly, a shape loomed in the shadows in front of him. Someone else must like to explore at midnight, too, Fievel thought. Slowly he crept closer. Now he could see who it was.

It was the stranger in the cowboy suit!

"Hey, I know you!" said Fievel. "You sold us the tickets. Are you going out West, too?"

The mouse had a strange wooden smile on his face. But he didn't move or say a word.

Fievel tapped him on the shoulder. "Hey, mister—"

The puppet tumbled into Fievel's arms. Fievel gasped and jumped back, tangling himself in the strings. He started to shout. Then he heard voices in the car below. Voices that hissed and meowed. His cry for help froze in his throat.

They were cats!

Fievel looked down. Several cats and one inky-black spider were playing cards by candlelight.

"I win again!" the tarantula said.

"Chula, you're a dirty rotten cheater!" said one of the cats. Fievel gasped. It was One-Eye, the cat that had chased his family into the sewer! Nearby, their elegant leader, Cat R. Waul, sat reading a book.

"I still don't get it, boss," said One-Eye. "How come we're not eating the mice?"

Cat R. Waul sighed. How many times would he have to explain it to these dimwits? "Of course we will eat the mice. But only after we have used them to do our work."

Fievel could hardly believe his ears. Slowly, carefully, he tried to free himself from the puppet strings. He had to warn the others!

"It is smarter to be nice to the mice," Cat R. Waul continued. "If we talk sweetly to them, they will fall into our hands. If we hiss and growl, they will run away. We will have to chase them. Such a waste of calories!"

"So when do we take the big bite, boss?" asked One-Eye.

Cat R. Waul smiled as he pictured the plans in his mind. "When my empire at Green River is complete—and we have built a better mousetrap!"

All the talk of mice had made Cat R. Waul hungry. Licking his lips, he opened his lunchbox and pulled out the squirming conductor mouse.

"Chula!" he called. "A little music with my lunch, if you please."

Chula cranked up a dusty old record player. He dropped the needle on a scratchy worn-out record. Flowery sweet music filled the train car. Most of the cats made faces and stuck their fingers in their ears. But Cat R. Waul smiled. He loved music almost as much as he loved mice.

He carefully laid the wiggling conductor mouse on a piece of white bread. Then he gently covered the mouse with a second slice, as if he were tucking him into bed.

Cat R. Waul closed his eyes and opened his mouth.

High above him, Fievel shoved the puppet off the ledge. The wooden mouse knocked the real mouse out of the sandwich—just as Cat R. Waul took a bite.

CRUNCH! Splinter sandwich!

Cat R. Waul howled as he spit out a mouthful of wood.

The conductor mouse scampered safely away. But Fievel was still stuck on the ledge. Cat R. Waul looked up. And then he smiled. "My, my, what have we here?" He tugged at the puppet strings and the tangled Fievel fell into his waiting arms.

"Why, it's a young mouse with ears bigger than my appetite," Cat R. Waul said, dangling Fievel by his tail. He dunked him into a jar of mustard.

"How delightful of you to drop in," he continued. "And just in time for my midnight snack."

Fievel closed his eyes in horror. But Cat R. Waul changed his mind. He knew if he ate this one tiny mouse, *all* the mice would get suspicious. His plan would be ruined.

Cat R. Waul dunked Fievel into a saucer of milk to wash the mustard off. There were better ways to take care of snoopy little mice.

"Run back to your parents," he told Fievel. "And do be careful." He winked at his cats. "It's a dangerous world out there."

Dripping with milk, Fievel quickly ran off before the cat could change his mind. But Cat R. Waul wasn't finished with him yet.

"Chula, take care of that mouse," Cat R. Waul ordered. "I don't want him talking. But make it look like an accident—and make sure his family sees the whole thing."

Chula hurried into the darkness. When he caught up with Fievel, he shouted, "Mouse overboard!"

Mouse overboard? Fievel thought. Where?

Then Chula pushed Fievel off the train!

Fievel's screams woke the other mice. They rushed over to help and found Fievel clinging to an iron bar beneath the train.

"Fievel!" cried Papa. He reached for his son, but Fievel's hands slipped. Mama hid her face and Tanya screamed as Fievel fell from the train . . .

And landed safely in the sand.

"I'm okay!" Fievel shouted to his family. "I'll find you in Green River!"

"Follow the tracks!" Papa called out.

"And don't forget to wear your hat," Mama shouted into the wind.

In seconds the train disappeared into the dark night.

And Fievel was all alone.

7

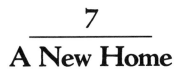

A New Home

Sadly the Mousekewitz family continued the journey without Fievel. They felt just terrible. But when the train chugged into Green River, they felt even worse.

Green River was not at all what they had expected. It was hardly a town at all. The general store looked almost empty. The town's only bank was closed—someone had stolen all the money! A tired old dog lay in front of the Sagebrush Saloon swatting flies in his sleep. And a sign on the door of the sheriff's office said, "Help Wanted."

Even worse, there was not a single cheese tree in sight!

"You know something, Papa?" Mama said as she slowly stepped off the train. "I think we got schnookered."

"No, Mama," said Papa, trying to keep up everyone's spirits. "This is what a land of opportunity looks like!"

Mama looked sadly at Fievel's bag. "It feels empty and lonely to me."

Just then Cat R. Waul and his gang of cats stepped off the train. Mama grabbed Papa's arm.

"Remember, Mama," whispered Tanya, "cats are nice in the West."

"Huh!" said Mama. "I'll believe that when I see it!"

Cat R. Waul walked up to Mama. He and his cats tipped their hats politely.

"I was sorry to learn of your son's clumsy accident, Madam," he said. "I'm sure he'll be along . . ."

"Yeah, one of these years!" snickered Chula.

Cat R. Waul frowned and jabbed the spider with his elbow. Then he added, "Please let me know if I can be of help during your time of sadness."

"Thank you," said Mama. "You're . . . very kind." She was still not sure whether to trust this strange cat or not.

Meanwhile, all the other mice hurried to claim the best spots for their new homes. One family ran under the saloon. Another set up house in a barrel. Others found homes under the general store.

"Hurry, Papa!" Mama said. "Or there will be no place left for us!"

Just then Papa spotted the town water tower. A stream of fresh clear water flowed from a small hole in the side. "You see," said Papa, leading the family toward the tower. "Everybody else is fighting over the land. But in this dusty country, you want to be near the water!"

Mama looked at the little muddy spot of dirt that Papa had picked out for their new home. "So," said Mama, "this is what we left New York for? This is what we . . . lost Fievel for?" She burst into tears.

"Don't cry," said Papa. "Fievel will come. And if we work hard, Green River will be everything we've ever dreamed of by the time he gets here. You'll see, with plenty of water—"

But Cat R. Waul had sent Chula up the water tower to secretly plug up the hole. The water stopped. Papa watched the last few drops seep into the ground.

"How can we survive without water?" cried Mama.

Cat R. Waul just happened to be there to help. He and his cats cast long shadows across the little crowd of mice. "My dear friends," he said, smiling, "there's no need for worry. What are neighbors for? To lend a cup of sugar, a saucer of cream . . . a pail of water perhaps?"

The mice chattered among themselves, their heads bobbing. The stranger had been right, they said. Why, cats out West were as nice as could be!

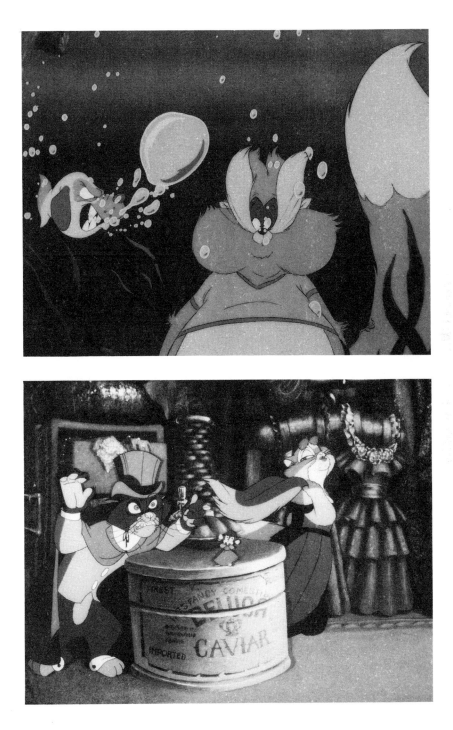

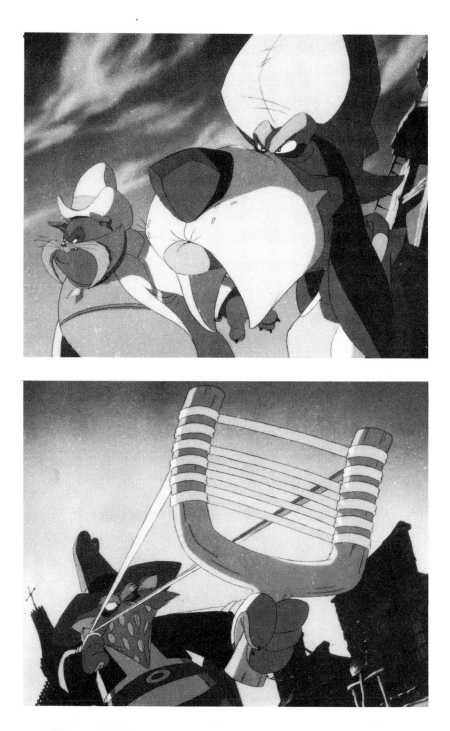

8

Tiger's Trip

Far away, Tiger was still swimming upriver. He was determined to find his friend Fievel—even if he had to cat-paddle all the way!

At last he spotted a riverboat with the words *Mississippi Belle* painted on the side. Ladies in colorful hoop skirts carrying lacy parasols flirted with handsome gentlemen as they strolled the decks.

Tiger grabbed hold of a rope that hung off the side of the boat. Hand over hand, he pulled his dripping body on board. Then he lay on the wooden deck, gasping for breath. Maybe he'd just catnap his way out West.

Finally Tiger opened his eyes. There was a dog bowl in front of his nose. And just beyond the bowl was a growling dog! "Not again!" Tiger said, sighing.

The dog chased Tiger to the very edge of the deck. There was nowhere for Tiger to go—but onto the boat's paddle wheel. It carried him up into the air like a Ferris wheel. But this ride didn't have safety bars. It didn't even have seats. As the wheel spun around it flung Tiger to a nearby shore.

Plunk! Tiger landed on the top of a jostling stagecoach. Now I'm really getting somewhere, he thought. Slowly, Tiger inched his way to the front, where a driver in a ten-gallon hat was whipping the horses into a gallop.

"Excuse me," said Tiger as he tapped the driver on the shoulder. "Would you by any chance be going to Green River?"

The driver turned around. It was a mean-looking Great Dane! Tiger jumped in fright and tumbled off the back of the coach. But just before he hit the ground, he got caught up by a loose luggage strap. He held on for miles as the stage bounced toward the open plains. But then the ground grew rougher and the trail grew sandy. When the stage hit a deep rut in the desert road, Tiger lost his grip and bounced to the ground. He tried to shout. But his mouth was full of sand.

With a sigh, Tiger stood up and brushed himself off. He looked around. He was surrounded by sand, as far as the eye could see. "What did I ever do to deserve this?" he moaned. "Lost—in a million-acre catbox!"

There was nothing else to do. So Tiger, the city cat, began to hike through the desert, wishing Fievel was by his side.

9

Desert Adventure

Miles away Fievel was following the railroad tracks. He had walked all day through the burning desert. He was hot and tired and thirsty. Day had turned to night. The desert grew cold. And still Fievel walked.

Would he ever see his family again? Fievel was no longer sure. He gazed up at the moon. It helped to think that Tanya and Mama and Papa—and even Tiger—were looking at that same moon, thinking of him, too.

Then Fievel saw a black shape outlined against the chalk-white moon. It was a giant hawk! The bird dove down to the ground. It wanted Fievel! The little mouse ran across the sands. But he could not escape.

Fievel felt the bird's huge claws curl around him. Then the hawk carried him up, up into the night sky.

Fievel closed his eyes as he dangled beneath the flying hawk. Nothing could be worse than this! he thought.

But he was wrong. A little while later, as the bird flew near a strange mountain, someone on the ground began to shoot arrows at it.

With a squawk, the hawk dropped Fievel and flew off into the night. Fievel tumbled toward the ground . . .

And landed in a huge platter of vegetables. "Yuk. Broccoli!" Fievel poked his head out of corn and beans—and looked into a huge mouth full of sharp teeth.

He was going to be somebody's dinner!

"Help!" he screamed.

"What in the world are you doing in the middle of my dinner?" said a voice.

Trembling, Fievel stared up at the creature who had almost eaten him alive.

It was Tiger, his friend from New York!

"Tiger!" cried Fievel. "I thought I was never going to see you again!"

Then Fievel realized he was surrounded by Indians. And they did not look happy about Fievel dropping in.

"What's going on?" Fievel asked his friend.

"Listen," whispered Tiger. "These Indians found me wandering around the desert. Now they think I'm something special. See that mountain over there? It's a sacred mountain. They think it looks just like me!"

Fievel smiled nervously at the Indians. Then he told Tiger what had happened on the train. "You've got to come with me to Green River," said Fievel. "I have to warn my family and all the other mice that the cats aren't really our friends. They want to turn us into mouseburgers!"

But Tiger was not so eager to go. He had never eaten so well in his life! "I don't know, Fievel," he said. "These folks may get offended if I eat and run."

Fievel couldn't wait. Sadly he said good-bye to his friend. Then he caught a ride with a tumbling tumbleweed and headed for Green River. He hoped he could get there in time!

10
Discovered

The next morning Fievel rolled into Green River. "Mama! Papa!" he shouted, running through the streets. At last he found his family and tumbled into their arms.

"It's a miracle you've come home!" Mama said with tears in her eyes.

"Fievel, what happened to you?" Tanya asked.

Fievel's words came out in a jumble. "First I got lost in the desert. Then a hawk caught me and dropped me into an Indian camp. And Tiger was there, and Papa—I have to warn you. The cats are not our friends. They're building a giant mousetrap to turn us all into mouseburgers!"

"Oh, Fievel!" said Papa, laughing. "The only thing growing faster than you are your tall tales."

"But, Papa, it's not a story!" said Fievel. "I heard them planning it."

"Come with me, young man," said Papa. "See for yourself. Out West the cats are our friends."

Beneath the human-sized Sagebrush Saloon, the mice were helping the cats build a much, much smaller saloon. And directly outside it, in the town square, a special stage was being set up. Everywhere Fievel looked, he saw cats *helping* mice. Fievel peeked around a cowboy hat lying on the ground. He saw a mouse with his arms full trip and fall. A cat brushed him off and helped the mouse to his feet. But still something did not look right to Fievel. Didn't that cat just smack his lips?

Suddenly a cat grabbed up the cowboy hat. Fievel clung to the brim as the cat plopped it on his head and hurried into the saloon.

Inside, Fievel heard familiar voices. He peeked out from under the hat. It was Cat R. Waul! He was going over building plans with his architect. At the same time Cat R. Waul was watching the stage. An endless stream of kitties took a turn singing, hoping to get a job at the saloon.

"The saloon will be finished tomorrow night at sunset," said the architect. "So here is the plan. We announce that we're going to have a special celebration—a grand opening in the town square. We invite all the mice and seat them in the stands. And when the sun goes down, our special stage will flip over and catch the mice in their seats. The world's biggest mousetrap!"

A screeching voice on stage made Cat R. Waul groan. "Terrible!" he cried. "What am I going to do? I must find someone whose voice is worthy of my wonderful saloon. Next!"

Another singer walked onto the stage and began

to sing. But just then Cat R. Waul spotted Fievel. "Well, well, well. If it isn't my little mouse friend from the train!"

"I heard what you said about the mice!" cried Fievel bravely. "And I'm going to tell everyone what a mean, rotten liar you are!"

"Are you now?" Cat R. Waul snatched up the tiny mouse in his furry paws. "Why, you're just a child. Whom do you think they will believe? Me or you?"

"Then I'll get Wylie Burp!" cried Fievel.

Cat R. Waul laughed. "Forget it, kid. I'm the law here. And you are merely . . . a light snack!"

There were no other mice in sight. So Cat R. Waul dangled Fievel over his mouth. Then he stopped as if hypnotized. The most beautiful voice he had ever heard drifted through the room like a spring breeze.

Cat R. Waul dropped Fievel at Chula's feet. "Save him for later," he said. "I've got to find out who's singing!"

Chula grinned at that most delightful order. He trapped Fievel inside a bottle and scurried off into the wings.

11

A Star Is Born

Cat R. Waul ran backstage. Desperately he looked around for the golden voice. Tanya Mousekewitz was on her knees scrubbing the floor. And as she worked she sang.

"A little mouse girl!" exclaimed Cat R. Waul. "You sing like an angel! Put down that scrub brush and bucket this minute. I want *you* to sing in my saloon." He picked Tanya up and held her gently in his hand. Then he carried her into a dressing room.

"Well, well, look what the cat dragged in." It was Miss Kitty, Tiger's old girlfriend. She was working in Green River now. "A mouse. How original."

"Not just any mouse," said Cat R. Waul. "This is the most beautiful singer in the world!" He set Tanya down on Miss Kitty's dressing table, staring at her as if she were a beautiful doll.

"You put a mouse on the stage and your saloon's gonna be empty," said Miss Kitty.

"They'll love her!" insisted Cat R. Waul. "Or they'll answer to me. Get her ready."

"Anything you say, boss," Miss Kitty said. Cat R. Waul blew her a kiss and left. But as soon as the door shut behind him, Miss Kitty let out a growl. And then she turned to Tanya.

Tanya was terrified. She backed up and stumbling onto a fluffy pink puff, got covered with powder. Tanya squeezed her eyes shut as Miss Kitty reached out her paw.

"Don't worry, mousie," said Miss Kitty. "You're safe now."

Tanya opened her eyes. Miss Kitty was smiling at her! "You mean you're not really tough and mean?"

"Who me?" Miss Kitty laughed. "Naw, I'm as soft as this powder puff and twice as gentle. But you've got to act tough around cats like that. You know what I mean?"

Suddenly Tanya froze. She heard the sounds of feet stomping and cat whistles out in the audience.

"It's time to face the music," said Miss Kitty.

But Tanya was terrified. "I've never sung before a real audience," she admitted. "And I'm not very pretty."

"Who says?" said Miss Kitty. "You can be whatever you want to be. You just have to believe in yourself." Miss Kitty shuffled through the pots and jars on her dressing table. At last she found just the right colors. Then she began to put makeup on Tanya's pale face. "Show me some grit and guts, girl. Come on. Give me a smile."

Tanya smiled weakly, teeth chattering.

Miss Kitty rolled her eyes. "No, no, no. You can do better than that! Think of something really nice. Reach deep down, and find the most beautiful thought in your heart."

"Well," Tanya said, almost whispering, "there was a young mouse back home . . . his name was Willie." Tanya smiled as she remembered him. Her face began to glow. Miss Kitty nodded as she helped Tanya into a fancy dress.

"Beautiful!" said Miss Kitty. "When you're on stage, imagine that Willie is sitting in the front row. Then sing your heart out, kid, just for him." Miss Kitty had a faraway look in her eyes, as if she were thinking of some place, and someone, far away, too.

"So what do you think?" said Miss Kitty at last.

Tanya looked into the mirror and gasped. "I look like a real lady!" she said breathlessly.

"Remember, though," said Miss Kitty. "The real lady is what's underneath the makeup. Now—go knock 'em dead!"

An audience full of cats restlessly waited for the show to begin. At last Cat R. Waul stepped out onto the stage.

"Ladies and gentlemen," he said. "Allow me to present the divine Miss Tanya!"

The crowd began to hoot and holler. The music began to play. Miss Kitty pushed a nervous Tanya out in front of the red velvet curtain. Tanya closed her eyes, took a deep breath, and opened her mouth.

Nothing came out.

12

Wanted: One Hero

The cats in the audience grumbled. Somebody in the back row snickered.

Tanya opened her eyes and stared terrified into the laughing faces. Then she imagined each one was Willie. Tanya smiled. The music swelled inside her and she began to sing. To Willie, who was hundreds of miles away, but who was here, too, in her dreams.

The noisy cats fell silent as Tanya's voice filled the saloon. Tanya looked at their faces. They were smiling. They liked her! Tanya could hardly believe it. She had never felt so wonderful in all her life. The joy in her heart filled her voice as it climbed higher and higher.

Backstage, Chula put two of his hands over his ears and scowled. He hated music!

Just then Tanya struck her highest note.

CRASH! Her voice shattered the glass bottle that held Fievel prisoner. He was free! He ran out onto the stage. Tanya was taking her bows before a cheering crowd.

Fievel grabbed his sister's hands. "Let's get out of here!"

But Tanya was in a daze. She saw only the smiling faces in the audience. She heard only their cheers. "I must stay," she said. "My fans need me."

"Oh, Tanya," said Fievel. "Your fans are cats. And they hate mice. We've got to warn the others!"

But Tanya wasn't listening. She just handed Fievel an autograph. Then she turned back to her audience and started to sing some more.

Fievel ran from the saloon. He looked around. He needed help, but he had no one to turn to. His parents didn't believe him. His sister was too wrapped up in applause to listen. He didn't know what to do.

"What's the matter, son?" Fievel looked at the old worn-out dog that lay in the gutter.

"Everything!" said Fievel. "Did you ever know something really important, but nobody would believe you? I need Wylie Burp!"

"You do?" said the old dog. "Well, then . . . he's right here. Right under your nose."

"*You?*" exclaimed Fievel.

"Read the badge, son," said the dog. "I'm Wylie Burp. At least, what's left of him."

"I need you, Sheriff Burp!" cried Fievel. "The cats are going to turn us all into mouseburgers! You've got to help!"

"I'm just too doggone tired," said Wylie. "Worn out from leading a dog's life. Sick and tired of fighting like cats and dogs every doggone day." The sheriff shook his head. "I'm just not the top dog I used to be."

Then Sheriff Burp looked at Fievel. His young face was full of hope and loyal admiration. It made the sheriff feel like a hero again. "Well, maybe I can help you anyway," he said.

"How?" cried Fievel. "We've only got till sundown tomorrow."

"Find me a dog," said Wylie. "I'll teach him everything I know."

Fievel's face fell. He didn't know any dogs. But then he smiled. He did know somebody he could get. Somebody who might work just as well.

13

A Dog's Life

Tiger was being hand-fed when Fievel ran into the Indian camp. "Tiger! You've got to come back to Green River with me!" he cried. "We need you to be a hero!"

Tiger mumbled through a mouthful of food, "Who wants to be a hero when you can have an all-you-can-eat buffet? Sorry, Fievel. You've got the wrong cat. I'm staying here. But please tell everyone hello."

"Too bad," said Fievel. "Because there's a very pretty kitty in Green River that you might remember."

"You mean Miss Kitty?" cried Tiger. "What do I have to do? I'll do anything—climb the highest mountain. Swim the deepest sea . . ."

"You just gotta be a dog," said Fievel.

"Forget it!" said Tiger.

But when Fievel met Sheriff Wylie Burp at Desperado Gulch the next morning, Tiger was with him.

The sheriff walked around Tiger. He looked him up and down. "Whoa-doggie! I sure got my work cut out for me!"

Then Wylie began to teach Tiger the cat how to be a dog.

Wylie threw a stick. "Fetch!" he barked.

Tiger waltzed across the sand. He leaned over and daintily picked up the stick. Then he carried it back over to Wylie. "Here you go!"

"Wrong, wrong, wrong!" shouted Sheriff Burp. "Let's try it from the top."

Sheriff Burp was a tough teacher. He taught Tiger how to walk like a dog. How to bark like a dog. How to think like a dog. He even rolled him in the dust to get him dirty as a dog.

All day long they practiced underneath the hot desert sun. More than once Tiger felt like giving up. But through it all, Fievel was there. "Come on, Tiger," he kept saying. "You can do it. We need you!"

Slowly Tiger began to act like a dog. At last Sheriff Burp was satisfied. Then he and Fievel disguised Tiger to make him *look* like a dog.

The Wylie Gang was ready. They headed into Green River for a showdown.

14

Showdown

The afternoon sun was slipping behind the rooftops of Green River as mice gathered in the town square. They were ready for a celebration. Cat R. Waul's saloon was finished at last! Dressed in their very best, the mice hurried to fill the stands.

Tanya stood with Miss Kitty on the saloon balcony and waved to Mama and Papa as they found their seats.

Everyone looked eagerly at the stage, where Cat R. Waul stood talking to Chula.

"Let's go over this one final time," Cat R. Waul whispered to the grinning spider. "First I will give a short but excellent speech. Then, as the sun sets, I will cut the ribbon. That will set this giant mousetrap into motion—and the mice will be ours!"

Chula banged the gavel as Cat R. Waul stepped to the podium. The mice shushed one another so they could hear.

"Cats and gentlemice," he began. "It is my pleasure to welcome you here today as we celebrate our greatest triumph. To mark this wonderful occasion, I hereby cut this red ribbon!"

The last rays of sunlight glinted on Cat R. Waul's golden scissors as he raised them in the air. But before he could cut the ribbon, a rock shot from a slingshot struck the scissors. They twirled into the air, and then landed in the dirt—

At the feet of the Wylie Gang!

"Cat R. Waul," said Sheriff Wylie Burp, "we've come to close you down."

"Well, well," said Chula. "If it ain't old Wylie Burp. I'd offer you some soap, if I didn't know you was already washed up."

"We're here to clean this town up," Wylie answered. "But I reckon it'll take more than soap to do it."

"Okay, gentlecats," said Cat R. Waul. "It looks like we're going to have to put these dogs through obedience school."

Cats came from all directions and pounced on the Wylie Gang. The mice in the audience watched in confusion.

"That's Fievel!" cried Tanya. "What's he doing?"

"And who's that dog with Wylie?" said Miss Kitty. "He's one heck of a fighter!"

"Chula!" hissed Cat R. Waul. "Trigger the mousetrap!"

As Chula hurried to obey, some of the curtains were torn from the back of the stage. Miss Kitty and Tanya looked down from the balcony and gasped.

"It's a giant mousetrap!" cried Miss Kitty. "They're going to flatten the stands!"

"What!?" cried Tanya. "Fievel was telling the truth after all!"

Tanya didn't think twice about her own safety. She left the balcony and rushed toward the stands. She had to warn the other mice!

Chula reached toward the ribbon.

"Now!" cried Cat R. Waul.

Just then a clear beautiful voice sang out through all the noise. Cat R. Waul stared out into the stands. Tanya was singing, trying to warn the others: "Oh say, can you see, you're on a mousetrap, so flee!"

"Stop!" cried Cat R. Waul. "You'll crush my beautiful singer!"

Tanya kept singing, loud and clear: "Run, run, run for your life!"

Mice started to flee the stands. But Papa raced to help Fievel. "When they attack one Mousekewitz, they attack all Mousekewitzes!" he cried. He rolled up his sleeves and joined the fight. Then suddenly Cat R. Waul pulled a gun on him.

"Freeze, you miserable vermin!" Cat R. Waul cried.

Everyone stopped. Mama stared in horror as Cat R. Waul cocked the trigger.

But then Fievel swung down on a rope. "Eeehaw!" he called out, as he knocked the gun from the cat's paw and sent it flying. A second later, Fievel was holding the gun.

Cornered, Cat R. Waul whined, "I—I was only joking."

Then they heard Chula shout, "Pull the ribbon, kid, or you've seen the last of Miss Kitty."

Everyone looked up. Chula had spun a sticky spider web around Miss Kitty.

Tiger, the soft cat with the gentle heart, growled. He attacked the cats like a real dog now. One by one he tossed them onto the stage as he tried to get closer to Chula. At last he stood right under the spider.

"You harm one patch of fur on her body," he said, "and I'll tear you apart—one leg at a time!"

Chula shot his web at Tiger. But Tiger grabbed the web and swung the spider in a dizzying circle above his head. When he let go, Chula sailed through the air. He landed with a squeak on the cat-covered stage.

And Miss Kitty dropped safely into Tiger's arms.

"Okay, Wylie!" shouted Tiger.

Wylie nodded. Then he called out to Fievel. "Let 'em rip, kid."

"Yessir, Sheriff," said Fievel. He shot the ribbon in two. The mousetrap sent the cats flying high into the air as it snapped harmlessly onto the empty stands.

Cat R. Waul and his gang landed in the mail pouch that hung by the side of the train tracks. The bullet that cut the ribbon had also put a hole in the water tower. And so the dirty water-hating cats got a long cold shower.

"MEE-YOWWWWW!" they hollered.

Then a whistle drowned out their howls as the mail train thundered through town.

"Nooooooo!" wailed Cat R. Waul as the mail bag was whisked away. The rest of his comments were lost in the wind.

The train sped off into the distance, taking the Cat R. Waul Gang with it.

"Hooray!" shouted Fievel. And he led the mice in a cheer that filled the town.

15

A New Life at Last

Mama and Papa hugged Fievel again and again.

"Fievel, my little Fievel!" cried Mama. "Can you ever forgive us for not believing you?"

"Of course, Mama," said Fievel.

Papa beamed at his brave young son. "You know, Mama, I'm just beginning to see that our 'little Fievel' is not so little anymore."

Fievel smiled proudly. Then he saw Tanya standing off to the side. "I'm a disgrace," she said. "I was so stuck on myself I forgot all about my family."

Fievel put his arm around his sister. "That's okay, Sis. You saved us."

"No—*you* saved us!" Tanya insisted.

Mama laughed and hugged them both. "So, I have a whole *family* of heroes!"

Suddenly Tanya stared at the train tracks. A small mouse family had jumped from the passing train. Now they stood looking around and brushing the dust from their clothes.

"Willie?" cried Tanya. She ran toward the young

mouse who had filled her dreams as she sang. "Willie, it's me!"

But the young mouse just stared at her. He didn't recognize Tanya in her fancy clothes and makeup.

Tanya quickly rubbed the makeup from her face. "Willie, it's me—Tanya Mousekewitz!"

Willie's eyes lit up as he recognized his old sweetheart. "Tanya!" he cried. He hugged her, and then they both blushed up to their ears.

Meanwhile, Tiger helped Miss Kitty out of the spider's web.

"You're one heck of a dog," Miss Kitty said in admiration. "Thanks for saving me."

Tiger laughed happily. Then he took off his disguise and became a plain old cat again.

"Tiger! It's you!" cried Miss Kitty. "And to think that I once called you a fraidy-cat!"

"Gosh, Miss Kitty," said Tiger. "I'm real glad to see you."

"Well, from now on, you're not gonna *stop* seein' me!" said Miss Kitty as she wrapped her arms around him.

Papa took out his fiddle. "Now it is time to celebrate!" he called to his family and friends. His bow flew across the strings and Tanya sang a lively Western tune that set everyone's feet a-dancing.

At last the Mousekewitzes' dreams of a new life were coming true.

61

16

A New Hero

Fievel and Wylie Burp stood on Prairie Dog Hill and watched the sunset. The colors were even more beautiful than they had been in Fievel's dreams.

Wylie took off his tin star. "Here, son," he said as he handed it to Fievel. "I want you to have this."

Fievel could not believe it. "I—I can't, sir. I'm not a hero like you. Not really."

"Maybe not," said Wylie. "But then again, maybe a real hero's the last one to know. You pulled me out of the gutter and got me back on my feet. And for that, son, I'll always be grateful."

Fievel smiled up at his hero as Wylie Burp looked out across the sky. "Just remember, Fievel," he said. "One man's sunset is another man's dawn. I don't know what's out there beyond those hills. But if you ride yonder, head up, eyes steady, heart open, I think one day you'll find that *you're* the hero you've been looking for all along."